GENETICALLY MODIFIED FOODS

KNOW YOUR FOOD

Fats and Cholesterol

Fiber

Flavorings, Colorings, and Preservatives

Food Safety

Genetically Modified Foods

Gluten

Organic Foods

Protein

Salt

Starch and Other Carbohydrates

Sugar and Sweeteners

Vitamins and Minerals

Water

KNOW YOUR FOOD

Genetically Modified Foods

MICHAEL CENTORE

MASON CREST

Mason Crest
450 Parkway Drive, Suite D
Broomall, PA 19008
www.masoncrest.com

MTM Publishing, Inc.
435 West 23rd Street, #8C
New York, NY 10011
www.mtmpublishing.com

President: Valerie Tomaselli
Vice President, Book Development: Hilary Poole
Designer: Annemarie Redmond
Copyeditor: Peter Jaskowiak
Editorial Assistant: Leigh Eron

Series ISBN: 978-1-4222-3733-5
Hardback ISBN: 978-1-4222-3738-0
E-Book ISBN: 978-1-4222-8045-4

Cataloging-in-Publication Data on file with the Library of Congress.

Printed and bound in the United States of America.

First printing
9 8 7 6 5 4 3 2 1

QR CODES AND LINKS TO THIRD PARTY CONTENT

TABLE OF CONTENTS

Key Icons to Look for:

Words to Understand: These words with their easy-to-understand definitions will increase the reader's understanding of the text, while building vocabulary skills.

Sidebars: This boxed material within the main text allows readers to build knowledge, gain insights, explore possibilities, and broaden their perspectives by weaving together additional information to provide realistic and holistic perspectives.

Educational Videos: Readers can view videos by scanning our QR codes, which will provide them with additional educational content to supplement the text. Examples include news coverage, moments in history, speeches, iconic sports moments, and much more.

Text-Dependent Questions: These questions send the reader back to the text for more careful attention to the evidence presented there.

Research Projects: Readers are pointed toward areas of further inquiry connected to each chapter. Suggestions are provided for projects that encourage deeper research and analysis.

Series Glossary of Key Terms: This back-of-the-book glossary contains terminology used throughout the series. Words found here increase the reader's ability to read and comprehend higher-level books and articles in this field.

SERIES INTRODUCTION

In the early 19th century, a book was published in France called *Physiologie du goût* (*The Physiology of Taste*), and since that time, it has never gone out of print. Its author was Jean Anthelme Brillat-Savarin. Brillat-Savarin is still considered to be one of the great food writers, and he was, to use our current lingo, arguably the first "foodie." Among other pearls, *Physiologie du goût* gave us one of the quintessential aphorisms about dining: "Tell me what you eat, and I will tell you what you are."

This concept was introduced to Americans in the 20th century by a nutritionist named Victor Lindlahr, who wrote simply, "You are what you eat." Lindlahr interpreted the saying literally: if you eat healthy food, he argued, you will become a healthy person.

But Brillat-Savarin likely had something a bit more metaphorical in mind. His work suggested that the dishes we create and consume have not only nutritional implications, but ethical, philosophical, and even political implications, too.

To be clear, Brillat-Savarin had a great deal to say on the importance of nutrition. In his writings he advised people to limit their intake of "floury and starchy substances," and for that reason he is sometimes considered to be the inventor of the low-carb diet. But Brillat-Savarin also took the idea of dining extremely seriously. He was devoted to the notion of pleasure in eating and was a fierce advocate of the importance of being a good host. In fact, he went so far as to say that anyone who doesn't make an effort to feed his guests "does not deserve to have friends." Brillat-Savarin also understood that food was at once deeply personal and extremely social. "Cooking is one of the oldest arts," he wrote, "and one that has rendered us the most important service in civic life."

Modern diners and cooks still grapple with the many implications of Brillat-Savarin's most famous statement. Certainly on a nutritional level, we understand that a diet that's low in fat and high in whole grains is a key to healthy living. This is no minor issue. Unless our current course is reversed, today's "obesity epidemic" is poised to significantly reduce the life spans of future generations.

Meanwhile, we are becoming increasingly aware of how the decisions we make at supermarkets can ripple outward, impacting our neighborhoods, nations, and the earth as a whole. Increasing numbers of us are demanding organically produced foods and ethically sourced ingredients. Some shoppers reject products that contain artificial ingredients like trans fats or high-fructose corn syrup. Some adopt gluten-free or vegan diets, while others "go Paleo" in the hopes of returning to a more "natural" way of eating. A simple trip to the supermarket can begin to feel like a personality test—the implicit question is not only "what does a *healthy* person eat?," but also "what does a *good* person eat?"

The Know Your Food series introduces students to these complex issues by looking at the various components that make up our meals: carbohydrates, fats, proteins, vitamins, and so on. Each volume focuses on one component and explains its function in our bodies, how it gets into food, how it changes when cooked, and what happens when we consume too much or too little. The volumes also look at food production—for example, how did the food dye called Red No. 2 end up in our food, and why was it taken out? What are genetically modified organisms, and are they safe or not? Along the way, the volumes also explore different diets, such as low-carb, low-fat, vegetarian, and gluten-free, going beyond the hype to examine their potential benefits and possible downsides.

Each chapter features definitions of key terms for that specific section, while a Series Glossary at the back provides an overview of words that are most important to the set overall. Chapters have Text-Dependent Questions at the end, to help students assess their comprehension of the most important material, as well as suggested Research Projects that will help them continue their exploration. Last but not least, QR codes accompany each chapter; students with cell phones or tablets can scan these codes for videos that will help bring the topics to life. (Those without devices can access the videos via an Internet browser; the addresses are included at the end of the Further Reading list.)

In the spirit of Brillat-Savarin, the volumes in this set look beyond nutrition to also consider various historical, political, and ethical aspects of food. Whether it's the key role that sugar played in the slave trade, the implications of industrial meat production in the fight against climate change, or the short-sighted political decisions that resulted in the water catastrophe in Flint, Michigan, the Know Your Food series introduces students to the ways in which a meal can be, in a real sense, much more than just a meal.

MODIFICATION METHODS

WORDS TO UNDERSTAND

artificial selection: when humans choose which plants and animals to breed, creating organisms with desired traits.

cross-pollinate: to combine the reproductive material of two different types of plants; it can happen on purpose or by accident in nature.

genes: units of inherited information passed from parents to children that determine different traits.

genetic engineering: the process of manipulating the genetic material of an organism, often by inserting new DNA into the organism.

genetically modified organism (GMO): a plant or animal that has had its genetic material altered to create new characteristics.

hemophilia: a condition where the blood is unable to clot properly, resulting in excessive bleeding even after minor cuts or injuries.

hereditary: something determined by genetic information that is passed from parents to children.

mutagenesis: when the genetic information of an organism is altered, either naturally or by exposing it to something that causes a genetic mutation such as radiation or chemicals.

pesticide: the general term for any substance used to kill unwanted organisms, including weeds, insects, and bacteria, that can damage crops.

Chances are you've eaten a **genetically modified organism (GMO)** today. Over 90 percent of large-scale agriculture crops, including soybeans, corn, and sugar beets, have been genetically altered in one way or another. Even if you didn't eat one of these products in its natural state, soy and corn are major ingredients in a variety of processed foods, and there's a strong possibility the sugar that sweetened your morning cereal was derived from beets.

Genetic modification remains one of the most divisive issues in modern food policy. The idea of humans "playing God" to manipulate nature can introduce strong emotional reactions and create controversy. Supporters and skeptics often cling to their arguments and cast doubt on each other's evidence. Looking closely at the myths, facts, and concerns of both sides can help us understand the role of GMOs, their potential benefits and drawbacks, and how they might impact the way we grow and consume our food for years to come.

GENETIC BASICS

GMOs are plants or animals that have had their genetic material altered by humans to give them specific characteristics or traits. Humans do this for all sorts of reasons, including making crops more resistant to **pesticides**, creating foods with higher vitamin and mineral content, and increasing crop tolerance to environmental factors like extreme temperatures or drought. GMO technology has also been used to produce seedless watermelons and grapes.

To understand how GMOs are created, it's necessary to know a little bit about **genes** themselves. Genes are made up of a material called deoxyribonucleic acid (DNA) that encodes the traits of all living things. In humans, genes determine our hair color, how tall we can grow, the strength of our eyesight, and the many different characteristics that make us who we are. These traits are passed onto us from our parents, meaning they are **hereditary**. Genes are located in structures called chromosomes that are found in the nuclei of our cells. The human body is estimated to have around 30,000 genes.

Some plants and animals have traits that help them survive better than those that do not have them. For instance, field mustard plants that flower earlier are able to survive shorter growing seasons brought on by drought. As plants and animals adapt to their environments over time, these desirable traits are transferred from one generation to the next. Eventually, they become widespread throughout the species. This process is referred to as *natural selection*.

MAKING SELECTIONS

Humans have been taking advantage of plant and animal genetics for centuries through a process known as **artificial selection**. Also known as selective breeding, this is when humans choose to grow specific seeds of plants with desirable characteristics, thus

Humans modify plants for many different reasons—for example, to create grapes that are easier to eat because they don't have seeds.

preserving those characteristics over time. A common example is corn: around 10,000 years ago, farmers in Mexico began saving and replanting the larger kernels of the wild grass teosinte. Over time, the cobs and kernels of the plant became larger and more plentiful, resulting in what we now know as corn or maize.

In fact, because of our experiments with artificial selection, much of the food we eat today looks nothing like what our distant ancestors ate. Humans have also selectively bred animals to create stronger, more productive offspring. Hybridization is the breeding of two genetically distinct individuals to create a new organism. It may involve breeding organisms from within the same species or between two different species.

Technically, selective breeding is a kind of genetic modification, in that humans are deliberately altering species to arrive at desired outcomes. The difference is that, in selective breeding, *all* the genetic material of the parent—both desirable and undesirable traits—is passed onto the offspring. With modern genetic modification, scientists can isolate individual pieces of genetic material for removal and replacement. They can also incorporate genetic material from one species into another, totally unrelated species, such

JELLYFISH PIGS

One of the more outlandish genetic modifications in recent years was the glow-in-the-dark pigs Chinese scientists created by injecting embryos with jellyfish genes in 2013. Some people saw these luminescent pigs as a dangerous (and even frightening) manipulation of an innocent species, but supporters pointed to the fact that the experiment was designed to research cheaper cures for human genetic disorders like hemophilia. The glow was used as visual proof that the genetic material injected into the embryo had been assimilated into the animal. In the future, scientists hope to use similar methods to produce beneficial enzymes (substances that start reactions) in animals that can be used as inexpensive medicines for humans.

The corn we enjoy today was bred 10,000 years ago by farmers in Mexico who began with a grass called teosinte and gradually created corn (maize) over time.

as a gene from an Arctic fish inserted into the genetic material of strawberries to help them grow in cold climates. This is not possible with selective breeding, where parent species must be similar.

METHODS AND MUTATIONS

In traditional selective breeding, scientists or farmers **cross-pollinate** plants to develop new ones with desirable traits. Sometimes this happens on purpose, such as when a farmer consciously decides to crossbreed two types of apple. Other times it occurs accidentally, such as when the wind carries pollen from one type of plant onto another. This is one way that wheat evolved from wild grasses. Ancient hunter-gatherers in the

CULTIVATING CABBAGE

Long before the advent of GMO technology, humans were modifying wild crops and selectively breeding animals in order to create new varieties. This is how six common vegetables—kale, Brussels sprouts, broccoli, cauliflower, kohlrabi, and cabbage—all came to be. All are derived from a single plant, the *Brassica oleracea*, or wild cabbage. It is native to southern and western Europe and likes to grow on limestone around the Mediterranean coast. Over the centuries, humans selected wild cabbages with different characteristics, bred them, and created new vegetables in the process. Kale came from breeding those cabbages with large, curly leaves. Brussels sprouts were bred from the buds on the plant's stem, and broccoli from the larger flowering buds at the top of the plant. These modifications are thought to be over 2,000 years old.

Wild cabbage is the ancient ancestor of quite a few veggies we eat today.

Fruit growers are continually developing new apples.

Middle East began harvesting, replanting, and cultivating wheat as a food source. They also crossbred different grasses to make stronger, higher-yielding wheat.

Today, breeders use something called "marker-assisted selection" to help them with cross-pollination. Instead of waiting years to see the (sometimes literal) fruits of their labor, they are now able to take a tiny sample of the new plant and screen its DNA. This gives them a "sneak peak" to see if the desired traits are taking hold, and it lets them determine which plants to continue cultivating and which ones to discard.

Scientists use a few different genetic-modification methods to develop new GMO crops. They may apply radiation to seeds or submerge them in chemicals. Both of these methods, forms of **mutagenesis**, cause genetic mutations within the plant's DNA. Scientists repeat the process over and over until they have created an interesting new trait. These methods are imprecise, but they can lead to some unique results, such as the Rio Red grapefruit. When this bright red variety was created in Texas in 1984, ionizing radiation was employed to create the color trait.

The "Ruby Red" grapefruit was the first grapefruit to be given a patent.

Mutagenesis methods are not regulated in the United States, and foods that have been altered with mutagenesis are allowed to be marketed as "organic." In Canada, those crops modified by mutagenesis are classified as GMOs, and in Europe the methods

MUSTARD MODIFICATION

With the looming threat of worldwide water shortage (see the *Water* volume in the Know Your Food series for more information), some scientists have been working overtime to find solutions that might salvage crop production. Many have explored genetic engineering. One Australian research team had success in 2015 with the modification of a species of mustard green. The team manipulated the gene that controls the number of pores, or stomata, in the leaves of the plant. Stomata control the movement of gases like carbon dioxide and oxygen into and out of the leaf. They also lose a lot of water through vapor. By modifying the gene to make fewer stomata, the scientists created a plant that uses less water while remaining hearty and productive.

Curly-leaf mustard greens.

cannot be used in organic farming. Genetic mutations can also occur naturally, such as when solar radiation from a hot climate or other environmental factors change a plant's genetic material over time.

HOW DO GMOs WORK?

Scan this code for a video about how GMOs are made.

GENETIC ENGINEERING

Because mutagenesis is so unpredictable, and because it has a low success rate for discovering beneficial traits compared to conventional breeding methods, it isn't widely used. Instead, the main way scientists create GMO crops is through **genetic engineering**. This is a type of genetic modification that is more precise and exacting. It is a four-step process:

1. *Identifying a desired trait.* Here, scientists find out what types of modifications farmers need in their crops. For instance, if there has been a prevalence of drought in recent years, farmers may need crops that can survive in low-water conditions. Scientists search low-water environments for plants with the desired characteristics, screening them to select the best options for genetic material.

2. *Isolating the desired trait.* Once scientists have selected the best options, they do the detective work necessary to find the part of the plant's genetic material that contains the desired trait. They might compare the plant to others of the same species that don't have the trait, or intentionally remove pieces of the plant's genetic material; when the trait disappears, they know which piece it belonged to.

3. *Inserting the desired trait.* With the genetic material removed from the plant, it's now time to insert it into the species being modified. If scientists have removed a trait that allows a plant to survive in low-water conditions, for instance, this is when they'll add it to the seeds of the crop they're trying to make more drought resistant. They can do this one of two ways: either shoot the new genetic material into the seed with a special "gene gun," or use a special bacteria as a "messenger" to insert the new DNA into the seed.

4. *Growing the new GMO.* After checking to see that the desired trait has been successfully transferred into the new organism, scientists begin the long and careful process of reproducing it with its genetic modification. They may use special temperature-controlled greenhouses, carefully track conditions, and inspect the modified plants by hand to ensure they are growing properly.

Some scientists describe this process as a bit like "cutting and pasting" pieces of genetic material from one organism to another. In reality, there are a few factors that make it a bit more random, such as the ability of the bacteria to successfully insert the new genetic material into the GMO. Also, new genes can move randomly around DNA stands, sometimes "turning on" undesired traits. Consequently, the transference of genes between vastly different organisms opens up the possibility of harmful, unplanned genetic reactions. The future of GMO creation depends on balancing these risks with the benefits that also come from emerging technologies.

TEXT-DEPENDENT QUESTIONS

1. What are genes made of, and where are they located?
2. Name one method of mutagenesis in genetic modification.
3. What are the four steps of genetic engineering?

RESEARCH PROJECT

Research a fruit or vegetable that, like corn, has been modified by humans through selective breeding or hybridization over time. Some examples include almonds, tomatoes, and grapefruit. Write a brief report summarizing the history of the fruit or vegetable and how humans have contributed to its development.

GMOs AND FOOD

WORDS TO UNDERSTAND

antibiotic: a medicine that kills harmful bacteria.

biofortification: the process of improving the nutritional value of crops through breeding or genetic modification.

ethics: a set of moral principles.

herbicide: a chemical designed to kill unwanted plants, such as weeds.

insecticide: a chemical designed to kill unwanted bugs that can destroy crops.

metabolism: the various chemical processes necessary to maintain a living organism.

patent: a license granted by the government that grants ownership of a new technology or invention, preventing others from producing or selling it.

In 2015 the world's farmers grew 440 million acres of genetically modified crops. This was down slightly from 2014, though the decrease had to do more with economic factors than a decline in interest in GMOs. Still, some researchers argue that GMO farming has begun to level off. Corn, soybeans, canola, and cotton dominate the global share of GMO crops. Few new crops have been introduced since the mid-1990s, due to a few different factors, including resistance from environmental groups, tightening governmental regulations, and some thorny technological limitations. A mere three countries—the United States, Brazil, and Argentina—are responsible for three-quarters of all GMO crops grown, and GMOs are still only a fraction of the world's total agricultural output. In 2013, 18 million farmers grew GMO crops worldwide—this might sound like a large number, but in fact it is less than 1 percent of the global farming population.

Yet in certain places—particularly the United States—GMO research continues, and GMO crops are widely used. The majority of corn, soy, canola, and sugar beets grown in the United States are genetically engineered. Since things like cornstarch and soy protein end up in processed foods, it is estimated that 60 to 70 percent of all the items on our grocery store shelves contain GMOs of some kind. With the exception of a few items, including papaya and squash, fresh fruits

A type of salmon was the first genetically modified meat or fish to be approved for sale in the United States.

and vegetables are not genetically modified. In 2015 the U.S. Food and Drug Administration (FDA) approved the first meat, fish, or poultry GMO product for human consumption: a type of salmon that has been engineered to grow faster than its non-engineered counterpart.

MODERN ORIGINS

The origins of modern GMO technology date back to the early 1970s, when two U.S. biochemists, Herbert Boyer and Stanley Cohen, discovered a way to snip pieces of DNA from one organism and transplant them into another. As other scientists began to experiment with the new technology, questions were raised about both safety and ethics. The global scientific community decided to hold off on further experimentation until they established safety guidelines in 1975.

In 1980 the first GMO patent was issued in the United States for bacteria that could consume crude oil in the event of an oil spill. The patent created a wave of interest among corporations in developing and owning GMO technologies. These technologies went on to impact the agricultural industry in major ways, including limiting the rights of farmers to save, reuse, and breed seeds that use GMO technology owned by corporations.

It was not until 1994 that the first commercially available GMO crop, the Flavr Savr tomato, was approved by the U.S. government for sale in grocery stores. The tomato was designed to have a slower ripening process, which kept it firmer longer. It sold well initially but proved too expensive to grow and ship, and production ended in 1997. But the Flavr Savr opened the market for other GMO food products.

FURTHER DEVELOPMENTS

In 1996 scientists unveiled the Roundup Ready soybean. The plant was modified with genes from the soil bacteria *Agrobacterium* that made it resistant to the

A tractor spraying a soybean field. "Roundup Ready" soybeans have been genetically modified to survive the application of herbicides.

herbicide Roundup. The active ingredient in Roundup, glyphosate, is very powerful; in addition to killing unwanted weeds, it can also kill neighboring crops. The GMO soybeans allowed farmers to use the herbicide around their crops without damaging the crops themselves. The genetic modification was repeated to produce "Roundup Ready" corn, cotton, and other plants. Today, around 90 percent of soybeans and corn grown in the United States are genetically modified to resist herbicides.

Also in 1996, the first generation of Bt corn came on the market. This was corn modified with another soil-based bacteria, *Bacillus thuringiensis* (or Bt toxin for short). The modification allowed the corn to produce proteins that protected it against insects. This meant that farmers no longer had to spray insecticides to ward off crop-damaging bugs. Plantings of Bt corn in the U.S. went from 8 percent of total corn acreage in 1997 to 79 percent in 2016.

PLAYING WITH NATURE

 GMO developers throughout the world are experimenting with more than just large-scale agricultural crops. Here are a few more specialized GMO foods:

- **The purple tomato.** This tomato is modified with genes from the snapdragon plant. The genes help the tomato produce an antioxidant called anthocyanin, which has a purplish hue and is found in blueberries. Studies have shown anthocyanin to have positive health benefits, including fighting inflammation in the body and even reducing the risk of cancer.

- **"Scorpion cabbage."** Back in 1994, scientists began experimenting with inserting the genes responsible for scorpion poison into cabbage—a pretty scary-sounding proposition. But scientists believe the poison will act as a pesticide to ward off harmful caterpillars, and they assure consumers that the toxin has been altered so it won't harm humans. Skeptics argue that the testing done has not been sufficient.

- **"Human" milk from cows.** In 2011 researchers in China inserted human genes into dairy cow embryos to make the quality of the cows' milk more like human milk. The change enhanced the protein content in the cows' milk, including a specific protein called lysozyme that fights infections in newborns. However, environmentalists and other anti-GMO activists are concerned about the effects of the modifications on both cows and people. Ten of the 42 genetically modified calves died shortly after birth, and six more died within six months of birth.

In addition to modifying herbicide- and insect-resistant products, scientists have turned their attention to biofortification, which is the process of improving the nutritional content of crops through breeding or genetic modification. The best-known example of this is Golden Rice, developed in 2000. This crop is modified with genetic material from daffodils and bacteria that allows the rice grains to accumulate beta-carotene, which is the source of vitamin A. Golden Rice is intended for countries where there are vitamin A deficiencies, which can cause blindness and increase the risk of fatal infections.

GMOs and Livestock

Besides corn, cotton, soybeans, beets, and canola plants engineered to resist insects and herbicides, GMOs are prevalent among a few other food products. Alfalfa, a crop in the pea family grown largely for animal consumption, is commonly modified to resist Roundup. Genetically modified alfalfa was deregulated in the United States in 2011, meaning farmers could buy it to feed their livestock. Dairy cows are the major consumers of GMO alfalfa in the United States; this means that their milk and milk-based products (like cheese and yogurt) technically contain traces of GMO ingredients.

Since products labeled "organic" cannot contain GMOs, organic farmers worry about the spread of GMO alfalfa to non-GMO, organic crops. This can happen when bees or other insects cross-pollinate, or move reproductive material, between GMO and non-GMO crops. Organic farmers cite the canola industry, where cross-pollination has negatively affected the organic market because of crop contamination.

Scientists claim the worry about cross-pollination is overblown. Farmers cut alfalfa hay before it goes to seed, reducing the probability of pollination significantly. And even if a rare occurrence of cross-pollination took place, scientists point to the fact that government regulations allow for low levels of pesticide contamination in organic crops and that many organic corn-based feeds contain small levels of GMOs.

Another GMO product that affects livestock is recombinant bovine growth hormone, or rBGH. Cows naturally produce bovine growth hormone, just like

While dairy cows are not themselves genetically modified organisms, many do consume modified crops.

humans produce growth hormones to help generate cell growth, development, and **metabolism**. In 1993 the U.S. Food and Drug Administration (FDA) approved the use of rBGH, a genetically modified version of bovine growth hormone designed to stimulate extra milk production in cows.

Despite the FDA's approval, there remains controversy around the use of rBGH. Some studies have shown that cows treated with rBGH have higher levels of a hormone called IGF-1, which has been linked to several types of cancer in humans. Some people worry that rBGH in milk will spark unnatural growth and early

Consumer pressure has made "hormone-free" milk more common.

puberty in the kids who drink it. However, this is untrue: rBGH is mostly destroyed during pasteurization and degraded in human digestion. It would have to be injected, not added to milk, to have any effect. Still, it is difficult today to find milk that doesn't have a "no rBGH" label—proof that distrust of the hormone (and fear of the potential risks of IGF-1) is persistent among consumers.

There's more conclusive data about the harm rBGH does to the cows themselves: those injected with it are more likely to contract mastitis, a painful infection of the udder. As hard as it is for the cows, this can also become a health problem for humans. To treat mastitis, farmers rely on antibiotics. The more antibiotics they

PAPAYA PROTECTION

In Hawaii in the mid-1990s, papaya farmers were battling the papaya ringspot virus (PRSV). This incredibly damaging disease had been around since the 1940s, but it had infected commercial farms with new strength by 1992. It deformed the fruit and its ability to reproduce. Farmers tried all sorts of methods to stop it, including killing infected trees, but nothing worked. Between 1992 and 1998, papaya production decreased by half.

A New York–based scientist named Dennis Gonsalves transferred a part of the gene from the virus into the plant, which protected it from PRSV. The new variety, dubbed the Rainbow papaya, saved the Hawaiian papaya industry and is still held up as a GMO success story. Some environmentalists, however, argue that the modifications have made the Rainbow papaya more susceptible to other diseases, such as papaya blackspot fungus.

Papayas ripening on a tree.

Scan this code for a video about the first GMO to hit the supermarket.

use, the more the bacteria in the cows build up a resistance to them. These antibiotic-resistant bacteria can create new "superbugs" that may transfer to humans. Plus, the residue of antibiotics in dairy products consumed over time may make humans more resistant to antibiotics overall. Some animal health professionals question the link between antibiotic use and superbugs, but the concerns are real enough that rBGH has been banned in Europe, Canada, and elsewhere.

APPLES AND POTATOES

Two more recent GMO crops to gain FDA approval are apples and potatoes. GMO apples are modified to reduce bruising and browning, meaning that they maintain their color long after you've bitten into one. Apples naturally produce an enzyme called polyphenol oxidase (PPO). When the cell of an apple is pierced—say, by biting or cutting—PPO mixes with other chemicals to produce a brownish pigment called melanin. By "silencing" the gene in the apples responsible for PPO production, genetic engineers were able to limit its production almost completely, meaning the apple won't brown.

The same technique was used to prevent bruising in the GMO potato. It was also modified to reduce the amount of a chemical called acrylamide that is produced when potatoes are cooked at high temperatures. In large doses, acrylamide can be cancerous to humans. In 2016, the FDA approved a second generation of the GMO potato that is engineered to resist a fungal disease that can wipe out entire crops.

This type of disease, or blight, was responsible for the Irish potato famine and other potato shortages throughout history.

Whether people will buy these new varieties is still up in the air. Both Frito-Lay, the country's largest potato chip manufacturer, and McDonald's, one of the world's biggest potato buyers, have stated that they will not be using the GMO potatoes because of safety concerns. Different genetic modifications can interact with one another and cause surprise side effects, some of which may be toxic to humans.

TEXT-DEPENDENT QUESTIONS

1. When was the first GMO patent issued, and what was it issued for?
2. What is Bt corn?
3. Name and describe two GMO food products.

RESEARCH PROJECT

Research one GMO food product that is widely considered a success and one that is considered a failure. Write a brief description of each product, how it was created, and the reasons why it has either succeeded or failed. Include issues related to human health, the environment, and the health of the animals or plants themselves.

JUST SAY NO TO GMO'S
These countries have BANNED Monsanto's GMOS.... Say NO! to GMO's in OUR Country!
1. Germany
2. Ireland
3. Austria
4. France
5. Switzerland
6. Japan
7. Australia
8. New Zealand
9. Mexico
10. India
thing
ur food

PROS AND CONS

WORDS TO UNDERSTAND

allergy: a condition where the body has a reaction (e.g., rash, itchy eyes, or swelling) to a specific substance.

carcinogen: something that causes cancer.

commodity crops: crops that are grown in large quantities and are easy to store and trade.

hybrid: something created by combining two different species or elements.

lymphoma: a type of cancer that affects the blood cells.

sustainability: whether a system or series of practices is able to be maintained for a long period of time without negative effects.

The debate around the creation, production, and sale of GMO food products can become complicated very quickly. There are many factors to consider, including the safety of GMO foods; the security of farmers to control, grow, and reproduce their own seeds; and the impact of GMOs on the environment, from increased pesticide use to the health of animals involved in genetic modification. GMO manufacturers, consumers, and farmers all have their own opinions on the place of GMOs in today's market. Meanwhile, the GMO debate—like many debates over the role of humans in modifying the natural world—can bring out strong emotions in people on both sides. This can cloud sound reasoning and make it harder to assess the evidence around GMOs.

"FRANKENFOODS"

Some people are naturally skeptical of what writers have termed "Frankenfoods," meaning foods that, like the legendary monster, are patched together out of different parts. A 2010 cartoon in which a genetically modified salmon with sharp, fang-like teeth and five eyes jumps out of a river to attack a bear captured the root of people's fears: that our attempts to engineer new species could upset the balance of nature and lead to dangerous consequences.

While scientists have yet to unleash bear-eating fish onto the world, the perception of GMOs as mutant, hybrid "Frankenfoods" has been difficult to shake. This is debated by certain scientists and food policy professionals who claim that GMOs are essential if we want to feed the world's exploding population, adapt crops to the growing threats of drought and climate change, and reduce our need for fertilizers and pesticides.

HEALTH CONCERNS

Health concerns are at the top of the list for anti-GMO advocates. They say that the technology has not been sufficiently tested on humans. Since it is so new, they argue, we do not have an accurate idea of how GMOs will impact human health. One anti-GMO website lists 65 health risks associated with GMOs. This may strike some as extreme, though at least a few of these concerns are legitimate.

Allergies are reactions certain people have to specific substances. Researchers estimate that 1 in 13 children have food allergies and experience symptoms such as rashes or difficulty breathing when they come in contact with nuts, wheat, shellfish, or other foods. Concern about GMOs and allergies first surfaced in the mid-1990s, when genes from the Brazil nut were added to soybeans to improve protein quality. Researchers found that the GMO soybean triggered reactions in people with nut allergies, and the product was not approved for sale. This led to more comprehensive safety testing to ensure new proteins introduced to GMOs do not cause allergies. Allergens (things that cause allergies) in GMO crops can spread to non-GMO crops through cross-pollination, so farmers must take precautions to ensure GMO and non-GMO plants are separated. Even so, it is very difficult to stop contamination entirely.

Many specialists say that the link between GMOs and the risk of allergies is overstated. Scientists point to the vast amount of research being done to identify proteins that may cause allergies at places like the AllergenOnline database in Nebraska. Others cite data showing that in the 20 years GMOs have been on the market, there have been no studies proving the connection between genetic modification and allergies. What's more, they argue, genetic modification

A sign from Portland, Oregon. Activists want agribusiness to be more transparent about their genetically modified ingredients.

THE PLIGHT OF THE MONARCH

Anti-GMO advocates often use the declining population of the monarch butterfly as evidence that GMOs are harming the environment. They claim that the increased use of herbicides due to Roundup Ready crops has allowed farmers to kill off weeds that other species require for survival. One of these, milkweed, is the only food monarch butterfly larvae will eat.

But GMO supporters argue that the issue is not so simple. They point out that even organic farmers try to remove milkweed because it is dangerous to grazing animals and disruptive to crops. They also argue that destruction of natural monarch habitats in Mexico and the effects of climate change have contributed more to the declining monarch population than herbicides or GMOs.

Pesticides are used to kill milkweed, which is the only food of the monarch caterpillar.

technology can even help *reduce* allergies by removing allergy-causing proteins from foods.

Another debated health issue is the connection between GMOs and cancer. A 2012 scientific paper found that a diet of GMO herbicide-resistant corn caused cancer in rats. However, questions about the research methods led to the paper being retracted the following year.

The health problems being debated may not be so much with GMOs themselves, but rather with the herbicides that farmers spray on them. Some GMO crops are engineered to resist herbicides, so farmers can use greater amounts to kill surrounding weeds. One of these herbicides, glyphosate (the active ingredient in Roundup), has been classified as a probable **carcinogen** by the World Health Organization (WHO). But even here, the science is not entirely clear. In 2016, for example, a joint study by the WHO and the United Nations found that glyphosate is unlikely to cause cancer from exposure through diet.

The debate over the safety of glyphosate continues with the growers who spray it. In May 2016, four Nebraskan agrarians filed a lawsuit against Monsanto, the manufacturer of Roundup, claiming that they were misled about the danger of glyphosate and that it contributed to them developing non-Hodgkin's **lymphoma**, a type of cancer. It was just the latest in a string of similar cases; in 2015 there were some 700 lawsuits pending against Monsanto over the alleged connection between Roundup and cancer. Monsanto has maintained that the product is not a human health risk.

Environmental Risks

Increased herbicide use isn't just a health issue; it's also an environmental one. Over time, weeds build up a resistance to Roundup, evolving into "superweeds" that can take over cropland. One possible solution to this problem is for farmers to rotate their crops every year, as different crops alter the soil composition in different ways,

A field of canola (also called rapeseed); there have been instances of genetically modified canola plants "escaping" from farms and growing in the wild.

making it harder for weeds to grow. This isn't always feasible on large-scale farms, however, so farmers have no choice but to increase the quantity and strength of the herbicides they use to kill the superweeds. More herbicides end up seeping into the soil and eventually running off into nearby ecosystems and water supplies. The United States Department of Agriculture (USDA) reported that GMO crops were responsible for an increase in herbicide use totaling 383 million pounds between 1996 and 2008.

PATENT LOGIC

Seed companies can sue farmers whose crops have been contaminated by patented GMO seeds for patent infringement, or using protected GMO seeds without paying for them. Monsanto claims that they would not sue farmers whose crops have been inadvertently contaminated by GMOs through cross-pollination. Such lawsuits would be impractical from a business standpoint, as the cost of legal fees would likely exceed the amount the company could win. This does not alleviate the fears of some farmers, who point to the fact that Monsanto has taken almost 150 growers to court and settled

The packaging of seeds states that the corn contains three patented genes to make the plants herbicide-resistant.

an additional 700 cases out of court. Monsanto responds that none of these cases involved patent infringement from inadvertent contamination.

Proponents of Roundup say that it has saved farmers from having to use stronger, more harmful pesticides, and that it has reduced the need to till the soil to eliminate weeds. Tilling can release soil rich in fertilizer and pesticides into the surrounding environment. Additionally, GMO supporters cite data that farmers have been able to reduce their use of insecticides thanks to crops modified with Bt toxin. There is concern that insects such as rootworms are beginning to develop a resistance to Bt crops, which could lead to increased insecticide use over time.

Gene contamination between GMO and non-GMO species is another possible environmental threat. This happens through cross-pollination, as in the example of alfalfa described in the previous chapter. GMO plants can also "escape" from farms into the wild. In 2010 ecologists in North Dakota found genetically modified canola plants growing on roadsides and other areas far from cultivated fields. Some of these plants had bred with each other to create new varieties with multiple genetic modifications. Ecologists worry that this "escaped" GMO canola could breed with wild weeds to create new herbicide-resistant superweeds, though many GMO scientists debate this. They say that, for the most part, wild weeds are unable to breed with GMO crops. Farmers who plant GMO crops are urged to place "buffer zones" between GMO and non-GMO seed, though the effectiveness of this method in preventing cross-pollination has been questioned.

THE BUSINESS OF FOOD

Other concerns over GMOs deal with food security: the agricultural practices, economics, and overall **sustainability** of a GMO-based food system. A main complaint about GMOs is that they reduce the diversity of crops planted on U.S. farms. GMO seed manufacturers such as Monsanto focus on developing large-scale **commodity crops** like corn and soy. These limited options are heavily subsidized by the U.S. government, encouraging farmers to grow them. This results in monocropping, or growing the same crop in the same place year after year, instead of

Wheat is commonly grown as a monocrop.

growing a diversity of crops and rotating them regularly. In 2014 the *Washington Post* reported that half of America's 300 million farmed acres were devoted to corn and soy, most of it genetically modified.

Monocropping can be a very efficient system, and it is more economical for farmers than crop rotation. It allows them to focus all their equipment, labor, and resources on an individual crop. But there are some negative aspects to monocropping that can surface over the long run. One is that it depletes nutrients from the soil, requiring farmers to use more chemical fertilizers. These fertilizers can further damage the health of the soil, seep into water supplies, and impact local ecosystems. Weeds and bugs adjust to monocrops more easily than they do to rotated ones, so these pests become harder to control without an increased use of pesticides.

GMOs also threaten to make genetic material within a species more alike over time. This limits genetic diversity, which is essential for the health of a thriving ecosystem. Without genetic diversity, organisms have a harder time adapting to changing environments. If a disease takes over a crop lacking genetic diversity, it can wipe out everything, since all plants share the same genetic information and susceptibility to the disease. This is what happened during the Irish potato famine of the 19th century.

A related criticism of GMOs deals with the way the agricultural business itself is set up. There is a high concentration of power in the hands of a few companies who develop, manufacture, and sell seeds to farmers. One of the largest companies, Bayer, made an offer to buy the other largest company, Monsanto, in 2016. Assuming the deal is completed, it will create the world's largest agricultural and pesticide company. This sort of business structure limits the options farmers have to buy non-GMO seeds. Critics fear that a reduction in competition will lead to higher

Scan this code for a video about the debate over Golden Rice.

prices, especially for poor farmers in developing nations. Smaller-scale plant breeders also may have fewer opportunities to sell other (possibly cheaper) seed varieties.

Many anti-GMO advocates are also disturbed by the fact that seed companies such as Monsanto can patent GMO seeds. A patent gives the company exclusive rights over how and where the seeds are used. Firms can even force farmers who buy their seeds to sign contracts dictating terms of use. A Monsanto contract, for instance, specifies that seeds be used only once and that farmers cannot save seeds from crops to replant the following year. But patents expire, leading to the creation and sale of "off-brand" GMO seeds that cost less and have no regulations on saving and replanting.

TEXT-DEPENDENT QUESTIONS

1. What is glyphosate, and is it considered harmful?
2. Have GMOs decreased the overall use of herbicides in the United States? Why or why not?
3. Name one advantage and one disadvantage of monocropping.

RESEARCH PROJECT

Research a recent GMO-related story in the news. It could deal with anything from an agricultural business merger to a newly developed GMO product or a legal case involving GMO labeling or patent rights. Write a brief synopsis of the article, including what you think it says about the future of GMOs.

RULES AND REGULATIONS

WORDS TO UNDERSTAND

biodiversity: the variety of living species in a place or ecosystem.

ideology: a collection or system of beliefs, theories, and ideas.

import: a product brought from one country into another for sale.

provision: something in a law or contract that states a specific action must occur.

regulatory: describing a policy, agency, or other entity that controls something through requirements or laws.

As the debate over the safety, ethics, and effectiveness of GMOs rages on worldwide, countries have developed different policies to regulate them. Some, such at the United States, have imposed mandatory labeling of GMO products, while other countries have banned GMOs outright. Proponents in developing nations encourage the adoption of GMOs to help feed growing populations, while detractors remain skeptical and advocate traditional farming methods. Though manufacturers, consumers, and policymakers alike sometimes see the issue in stark black-and-white terms, GMO development and regulation remain complicated topics. The science is still very new, and we are only beginning to learn how to navigate its future in our food supply.

RULES AND REGULATIONS

It can take an average of 13 years and $130 million of research and development costs for a GMO to go from a laboratory to a supermarket. Getting **regulatory** approval from relevant government agencies can take three years alone. There are more than 90 governmental bodies in the world that review and approve GMOs, and many countries have numerous agencies devoted to the project.

In the United States, three separate agencies are involved in the regulation of GMO crops: the USDA, the FDA, and the Environmental Protection Agency (EPA). The USDA looks at the GMO from an agricultural standpoint: whether a crop is safe to grow. They test to see whether it will become a "pest plant" by crossbreeding with nearby weeds, and evaluate any other problems it might have adapting to its environment. The EPA handles pesticide-related issues, including the ways that crops modified to resist herbicides or with Bt toxin might affect nearby plants and animals. Finally, the FDA is responsible for anything related to the crop as a food product, including how the GMO version of an item compares with a non-GMO one, the potential for the crop to transmit allergies or viruses, and other food-safety issues. The FDA also has the power to recall products they deem unsafe for people to eat.

Before a GMO is submitted for review, companies have to perform their own series of tests to ensure the product is engineered correctly, that it has the intended traits, and that it meets certain safety requirements. GMO developers may conduct more than 75 different tests in laboratories and outdoor environments. They also analyze the nutritional content of GMO products. The entire process can take up to seven years.

Critics of the GMO regulatory process in the United States believe it isn't effective. They say there are not enough studies done on the long-term effects of GMOs on humans. They also say that new technologies, such as the ability to modify plants without using foreign genes, have created loopholes that make it easier for companies to dodge regulations. Additionally, the regulatory process is so

Horticulturalists with the Agricultural Research Service (part of the Department of Agriculture)
collect an experimental type of plum that was developed to resist disease.

THE "MONSANTO PROTECTION ACT"

In 2013 a section of spending bill signed into law by President Obama caused an uproar. A section of the bill known as the Farmer Assurance Provision took away the power of federal courts to stop the sale and planting of GMO seeds, even if safety tests showed potential health concerns. This part of the bill was quickly dubbed the "Monsanto Protection Act" by anti-GMO critics, who were furious that the bill had been written with Monsanto's input. A petition against it drew 250,000 signatures, and as many as 2 million people participated in "March Against Monsanto" protests worldwide in May 2013. The public outcry worked, and the provision was removed from the bill in September.

This protest in Vancouver, Canada, was one of many that took place in May 2013, in reaction to the so-called Monsanto Protection Act.

expensive and time-consuming that only the wealthiest agricultural corporations can afford it, giving them greater power over the food supply.

INTERNATIONAL POLICIES

Not all countries are as welcoming of GMOs as the United States. In 2015, 19 countries from the European Union imposed a ban on cultivating eight new GMO crops within their borders. One of these, a type of GMO corn, had already been approved for cultivation by the European Union. At the same time, GMO imports are still allowed within the European Union; some 30 million tons of corn- and soy-based animal feeds are imported annually, much of them genetically modified.

In February 2016, Russia banned imports of U.S. corn and soybeans due to GMO contamination. Later the same year, the country officially banned both the cultivation and importation of all GMO products. The only exceptions are for those GMOs that are used in scientific research.

GMO policy in developing nations can be very conflicted. In 2016 the European Union opposed a large-scale agriculture effort in Africa that would use GMO technology. Those who supported the decision say that GMOs would reduce biodiversity, put small farmers out of business, and benefit big business more than local residents. Critics of the decision say it thwarts plans to reduce poverty and hunger across Africa, and puts ideology above the potential food security of millions of people.

African residents in countries such as Zimbabwe remain divided over the issue of GMOs. Some see biotechnology companies and genetic modification as inherently negative, almost evil forces. Others see widespread drought and other effects of climate change as a reason to begin adopting new GMO technologies that could bring higher yields of food at lower cost. University students in Kenya protested that country's ban on GMOs at the end of 2016, but for a slightly different reason: they felt that the ban weakened their chances for a career in biotechnology and that years of study would be wasted if they were not allowed to pursue biotechnology professionally.

LAWS AND LABELS

Beyond the cultivation, importation, and exportation of GMOs, a big part of GMO policy is labeling food products that contain genetically modified ingredients. Supporters of labeling say it protects the health and safety of consumers by making them aware of what they're eating. Opponents claim that labels overstate the danger of GMOs and drive up production costs for food manufacturers, which raises prices at the grocery store.

The GMO labeling issue has been at the forefront of U.S. food policy for the past several years. It began in 2013, when Connecticut became the first state to pass a labeling law. But the law contained a **provision** stating that it would only go into effect if a bordering state passed a labeling law, too, so it wasn't immediately effective. Maine passed a law like Connecticut's in 2014 with a similar provision. It wasn't until May 2014 that a third New England state, Vermont, passed a law with no provisions whatsoever: all foods containing genetically modified

CHIPOTLE

The fast-food burrito chain Chipotle tried to align with the anti-GMO movement in 2015, when it announced the start of its "G-M-Over It" campaign. The campaign stated that Chipotle had removed all GMO ingredients from its products. However, this was later contested in court when Chipotle customers argued that the meat, cheese, and sour cream Chipotle served came from animals raised on GMO feeds. Customers also said they had been charged more because the food was supposedly non-GMO. Chipotle denied the accusations, saying they had been open about the sources of their animal products and not raised prices. The case was dismissed in November 2016.

A GMO labeling protest in North Carolina.

Scan this code for a report about GMOs in Europe.

ingredients would have to be labeled. The Vermont law took effect in 2016, but it was soon overturned by the passage of a national bill governing GMO labeling.

The U.S. Congress passed its own GMO labeling bill in 2015, called the Safe and Accurate Food Labeling Act. This removed mandatory labeling requirements for food manufacturers, but gave the FDA authority to require labels under certain conditions, such as if a genetically modified food contained a known allergen. Defenders of the bill said that it was better to have a single, unified law rather than different laws for different states, while opponents claimed it didn't go far enough. The bill did not pass in the Senate, however, and was not signed into law.

There were further developments the following year, when corporations such as General Mills began labeling foods with genetically modified ingredients. In the U.S. Congress, the House of Representatives and the Senate proposed different ways to solve the labeling debate. A compromise was finally reached in July 2016, and President Barack Obama signed a national GMO labeling bill into law. A major criticism of the new national law is that companies do not have to use a clearly identifiable label on GMO products; instead, they can use a Quick Response (QR) code that customers can scan with their smartphones (like how you scan for videos in this book) to get further information. Critics believe this makes the labeling process too complicated and hides important information from people who may not have access to a smartphone.

THE WAY AHEAD

There are no easy answers in the GMO debate. Some researchers say we have arrived at a time where climate change, population growth, and other factors have necessitated the adoption of new technologies to feed our world. On the other hand, anti-GMO activists have made an influential case for further testing to ensure that GMOs are safe for humans and not contributing to allergies, antibiotic resistance, and other health issues.

As producers, consumers, and government officials try to figure out the best policies regarding GMOs, people from environmental, agricultural, scientific, and other backgrounds have proposed different ways to reshape our food system. Some are economic, such as ensuring that farmers have access to inexpensive seeds, or that agricultural corporations are not allowed to become so large as to dominate the entire market. Others involve governmental oversight, like public funding for

Many people associate GMOs with the fruit and vegetable aisle, but in fact they are in many of the processed foods we consume every day.

breeding programs that make seeds more compatible with local ecosystems, or a reduction in the amount of GMO corn grown for ethanol fuel. Still others are aimed at consumers, such as reducing our intake of processed foods that are heavily dependent on GMO corn and soy, or cutting back on food waste overall. It is estimated that waste accounts for an alarming 30 to 40 percent of food production.

Beyond these suggestions, some scientists and food activists have proposed a more equal regulatory system between GMO and non-GMO products. Such a system would look at the end result of each product: how it works with local economies and environments, the benefits of its new traits, and other qualities. Those in favor say that the line between genetic engineering and conventional breeding is not as clear as it once was because of new technology, and that either technique can introduce harmful traits. They argue that it is ultimately safer to test and regulate the newly created traits, rather than the breeding methods.

TEXT-DEPENDENT QUESTIONS

1. What are the three U.S. organizations involved in regulating GMOs?
2. What is a criticism of the GMO labeling law passed in the United States in 2016?
3. Name two potential strategies people have suggested for reshaping our food supply system.

RESEARCH PROJECT

Select three countries around the world and research their positions on GMOs, including policies within the country, regulations on imports and exports, and public opinion. Write a brief report comparing and contrasting the different positions.

FURTHER READING

BOOKS AND ARTICLES

Callis, Tom. "Papaya: A GMO Success Story." *Hawaii Tribune-Herald*, June 10, 2013. http://hawaiitribune-herald.com/sections/news/local-news/papaya-gmo-success-story.html.

"Genetically Modified Foods." *FactMonster*. http://www.factmonster.com/ipka/A0933209.html.

Hakim, Danny. "Doubts about the Promised Bounty of Genetically Modified Crops." *New York Times*, October 29, 2016. https://www.nytimes.com/2016/10/30/business/gmo-promise-falls-short.html?_r=0.

Jenkins, McKay. *Food Fight: GMOs and the Future of the American Diet*. New York: Avery, 2017.

Saletan, William. "Unhealthy Fixation." *Slate*, July 15, 2015. http://www.slate.com/articles/health_and_science/science/2015/07/are_gmos_safe_yes_the_case_against_them_is_full_of_fraud_lies_and_errors.html.

Shetterly, Caitlin. *Modified: GMOs and the Threat to Our Food, Our Land, Our Future*. New York: G. P. Putnam's Sons, 2016.

WEBSITES

Genetic Literacy Project

www.geneticliteracyproject.org

This comprehensive website is dedicated to advances and potential drawbacks of genetic technology, with a special section on food and agriculture.

MIT Technology Review

www.technologyreview.com

The Massachusetts Institute of Technology publishes this magazine in print and online, with in-depth articles on biotechnology, robotics, renewable energy, and more.

Modern Farmer

lmodernfarmer.com

With articles covering everything from technology to food policy to various "how to" guides, the website for the magazine *Modern Farmer* has information for anyone interested in today's agriculture.

EDUCATIONAL VIDEOS

Chapter One: GMO Answers. "How Are GMOs Created?" https://www.youtube.com/watch?v=2G-yUuiqIZ0.

Chapter Two: *New York Times*. "You Call That a Tomato?" http://www.nytimes.com/2013/06/24/booming/you-call-that-a-tomato.html.

Chapter Three: Reuters. "'Golden Rice' Galvanizes Both Sides of Philippines Food Fight." https://www.youtube.com/watch?v=U02ohdFLe10.

Chapter Four: European Parliament. "Europe's New Approach to GMOs." https://www.youtube.com/watch?v=OpYQf1Kas8U.

SERIES GLOSSARY

amino acid: an organic molecule that is the building block of proteins.

antibody: a protein in the blood that fights off substances the body thinks are dangerous.

antioxidant: a substance that fights against free radicals, molecules in the body that can damage other cells.

biofortification: the process of improving the nutritional value of crops through breeding or genetic modification.

calories: units of energy.

caramelization: the process by which the natural sugars in foods brown when heated, creating a nutty flavor.

carbohydrates: starches, sugars, and fibers found in food; a main source of energy for the body.

carcinogen: something that causes cancer.

carnivorous: meat-eating.

cholesterol: a soft, waxy substance present in all parts of the body, including the skin, muscles, liver, and intestines.

collagen: a fibrous protein that makes up much of the body's connective tissues.

deficiency: a lack of something, such as a nutrient in one's diet.

derivative: a product that is made from another source; for example, malt comes from barley, making it a barley derivative.

diabetes: a disease in which the body's ability to produce the hormone insulin is impaired.

emulsifiers: chemicals that allow mixtures to blend.

enzyme: a protein that starts or accelerates an action or process within the body.

food additive: a product added to a food to improve flavor, appearance, nutritional value, or shelf life.

genetically modified organism (GMO): a plant or animal that has had its genetic material altered to create new characteristics.

growth hormone: a substance either naturally produced by the body or synthetically made that stimulates growth in animals or plants.

herbicide: a substance designed to kill unwanted plants, such as weeds.

ionizing radiation: a form of radiation that is used in agriculture; foods are exposed to X-rays or other sources of radiation to eliminate microorganisms and insects and make foods safer.

legume: a plant belonging to the pea family, with fruits or seeds that grow in pods.

macronutrients: nutrients required in large amounts for the health of living organisms, including proteins, fats, and carbohydrates.

malnutrition: a lack of nutrients in the diet, due to food inaccessibility, not consuming enough vitamins and minerals, and other factors.

marketing: the way companies advertise their products to consumers.

metabolism: the chemical process by which living cells produce energy.

micronutrients: nutrients required in very small amounts for the health of living organisms.

monoculture farming: the agricultural practice of growing a massive amount of a single crop, instead of smaller amounts of diverse crops.

nutritional profile: the nutritional makeup of given foods, including the balance of vitamins, minerals, proteins, fats, and other components.

obesity: a condition in which excess body fat has amassed to the point where it causes ill-health effects.

pasteurization: a process that kills microorganisms, making certain foods and drinks safer to consume.

pesticide: a substance designed to kill insects or other organisms that can cause damage to plants or animals.

processed food: food that has been refined before resale, often with additional fats, sugars, sodium, and other additives.

protein complementation: the dietary practice of combining different plant-based foods to get all of the essential amino acids.

refined: when referring to grains or flours, describing those that have been processed to remove elements of the whole grain.

savory: a spicy or salty quality in food.

subsidy: money given by the government to help industries and businesses stay competitive.

sustainable: a practice that can be successfully maintained over a long period of time.

vegan: a person who does not eat meat, poultry, fish, dairy, or other products sourced from animals.

vegetarian: a person who does not eat meat, poultry, or fish.

whole grain: grains that have been minimally processed and contain all three main parts of the grain—the bran, the germ, and the endosperm.

INDEX

ABOUT THE AUTHOR

Michael Centore is a writer and editor. He has helped produce many titles, including memoirs, cookbooks, and educational materials, for a variety of publishers. He has authored numerous books for Mason Crest, including titles in the Major Nations in a Global World and Drug Addiction and Recovery series. His work has appeared in the *Los Angeles Review of Books, Killing the Buddha, Mockingbird,* and other print- and web-based publications. He lives in Connecticut.

PHOTO CREDITS